THE NOT-SO-

PERFECT

PLANET

WAY-
TOO-REAL
ALIENS

#2

THE NOT-SO-
PERFECT
PLANET

PAMELA F. SERVICE · ILLUSTRATIONS BY MIKE GORMAN

Text copyright © 2012 by Pamela F. Service
Illustrations copyright © 2011 by Lerner Publishing Group, Inc.

Darby Creek
A division of Lerner Publishing Group, Inc.
241 First Avenue North
Minneapolis, MN 55401 U.S.A.

Website address: www.lernerbooks.com

Main body text set in ITC Officina Sans Std Book 12/18
Typeface provided by International Typeface Corp

Library of Congress Cataloging-in-Publication Data

Service, Pamela F.
        The not-so-perfect planet / by Pamela F. Service ; illustrated by Mike Gorman.
            p.   cm.— (Way-too-real aliens ; #2)
        Summary: Aspiring author Josh writes about an ideal vacation planet, hoping that he and his sister Maggie can travel to outer space safely and have summer fun, but he does not count on encountering the creatures that are already living there.
        ISBN 978-0-7613-7919-5 (trade hard cover : alk. paper)
        [1. Extraterrestrial beings—Fiction. 2. Interplanetary voyages—Fiction. 3. Brothers and sisters—Fiction. 4. Science fiction.] I. Gorman, Mike, ill. II. Title.
    PZ7.S4885No 2012
    [Fic]—dc23   2011016409

Manufactured in the United States of America
1 – SB – 12/31/11

FOR WANDA, MARCIA, AND KATHY

CHAPTER ONE

BROCHURE DREAMS

Little sisters are, by definition, a pain. My sister Maggie has been a *maximum* pain ever since our adventure with the blue guys.

She's the one who calls it an adventure, by the way. I call it a really scary time when we could have been killed, and I don't want to do it again. And that's the problem. She *does* want to do it again.

I'd better fill you in. I wrote the winning story for a school writing contest. It got published (well, printed) and sold in the local bookstore. Some creepy blue aliens read it and tracked me down. They explained that humans are "actualizers." We're one of the few species in the universe who write fiction. But it's really not fiction— we tune into real worlds that exist somewhere else. The writer describes them without even knowing it.

Yeah, I know—sounds weird. And it gets weirder.

These blue guys wanted to find the world from my story—the world I thought I'd made up. They plunked a crownlike gizmo on my head that transported me, Maggie, and their gang away from Earth. I won't tell you everything that happened next, but the planet had sharp swords, traitorous priests, giant spider-things, and lava monsters, and it was really, really dangerous. When we finally managed to get back home, I said I never wanted to use the gizmo again. I hid it.

Lot of good that did me.

Maggie kept bugging me about it. Whenever our parents weren't looking, she'd ring her hands around her head like a crown. And whenever we were really alone, she'd badger me with bogus arguments about how we could try it again, have lots of fun, and be perfectly safe. No way.

I tried to keep away from her. Like one Saturday I was in the woods, making what I thought was a secret fort. An awesome creation, if I do say so myself. Not kid stuff either—this was sophisticated. I built a fence of fallen branches around a big tree stump, then hammered in ladder rungs up a tree that had spouted from the old stump. Near the top, I nailed together wooden planks to make a crow's nest.

So there I was in my watchtower, scanning the woods for imaginary enemies. Then I heard snickering below. From within the safe walls of my secret fort, Maggie grinned up at me.

"Josh, don't be such a bore. Instead of playing, you could be having real adventures. *We* could be."

I wanted to banish her from my fort right then. But what was the point? As a secret hideout, it was finished. "You don't get it," I said. "Pretend adventures are *safe* adventures. That world my story took us to was *real*, and we could have gotten really dead."

She snorted. "That's because you wrote that story to win a contest. You put in lots of dangerous stuff so it'd be exciting. But you're not really imagining a world when you're writing, right? So write a nice story! Tune into a place that's not so scary."

I snorted back, feigning interest in a noisy raven overhead. "Too risky."

"Not if you work it all out carefully ahead of time," Maggie said. "Look, Mom and Dad said we can't afford a fancy vacation this summer. So let's create a vacation of our own! Think of some really pretty place like on those travel brochures Dad's always drooling over. You know, white beaches, blue sea, exotic flowers . . ."

"Yeah, probably lots of bloodthirsty beasts too."

"Why? There's got to be a really nice vacation planet somewhere. Write about it, put that gizmo on, and we'll find it."

I guess all her nagging finally wore me down. Her idea started to sound not totally stupid. Since our parents had said that we had to "tighten our belts," it was looking like a pretty boring summer coming up. *If I can write about a totally nice, safe world,* I thought, *maybe we could zap there for a few days. Then I could think us back to Earth, to the moment after we'd left.*

I didn't like making Maggie think that she'd won. But I'd seen those cool travel brochures too. "Okay," I grumbled, climbing down to meet her on the stump.

"But we've got to do this right. We've got to plan. Details make all the difference. We learned that last time."

For a while we sat on the stump, tossing around ideas for the perfect planet. I had to squelch a lot of hers. Elves? Come on. Hadn't she read any of those stories where elves are kind of scary?

After dinner, I sat in front of my computer, trying to hammer out a rough story idea. Despite the *KEEP OUT* signs plastered all over my door, Maggie burst in, perched herself over my shoulder, and suggested more dumb ideas. I'd beaten back several of them before she asked, "Well, if you won't put in talking flowers or wood elves, how about unicorns?"

I groaned. Her room is festooned with sickly sweet purple-and-pink unicorns and winged horses. But since I'd already turned down a bunch of her suggestions, I figured I'd better give her something.

"Okay, unicorns. But no flying horses."

"Why not? A herd of pegasuses would be so cool!"

"Yeah, but they could drop horse poop on you from the sky or trample you with their hooves. And if you decided to ride one, you could fall off—from way up in the air!"

"But I *liiike* flying horses!" she whined.

"And I like dinosaurs, but I don't want to visit a planet where they live for real."

Maggie was pouting by that point. I'm used to it. I didn't weaken.

"Okay," she said finally, "no flying horses. How about mermaids?"

Before I could object, she continued: "Come on, we agreed on white sand beaches and a sparkling green sea. Why not have mermaids in the waters?"

"Okay, okay. Mermaids. I don't plan to go swimming anyway. Now get out! I've got to think. We need to get this exactly right."

Finally, she left, a smug I-got-my-way look on her face. True, I didn't plan to go swimming on this world. Mostly I wanted to lie on that white beach, soak up the rays (no harmful radiation, I noted), collect shells, and look at the exotic wildlife. I also noted that the beaches didn't have anything that stung or ate people.

Then I began to worry. The planet sounded relaxing but kind of dull. The famous authors my school brings in to talk to us always say that a story has to have something *happen* in it or else it's not a story. *Does the alien travel-circlet only work on stories?* I wondered. *Maybe it won't work if I just describe a nice place to visit.* And I was just planning a *short* story, not a big novel. I hoped that didn't matter.

Anyway, to be safe, I figured I'd put in something exciting that could happen on that world. Not *dangerous*—no fierce, people-hunting things. But maybe fun stuff that characters could hunt for. *Jewels! Or at least pretty stones,* I thought. *That'll do it. The planet can have lots of beautiful stones lying around.*

I got to work.

Of course, there was homework and TV and stuff, so I couldn't pour a lot of time into the story. But in a few days I was finished. After breakfast, I plopped a printout in front of Maggie. She shoved aside a jam jar and started reading, leaving strawberry jam smudges on the white paper. I surprised my mom by voluntarily cleaning up the breakfast dishes while my super-critical sister read on.

A few minutes later, she'd finished and headed for the back porch. Nervously, I followed.

"Well?" I said as she plunked herself on the porch swing.

"Kind of a lame story."

I fumed. "This isn't for a writing contest! It's a story about a world that would be fun and safe to visit, remember? Besides, you don't have to come if you don't want to."

She tossed my story back to me. "Oh, I'm coming. I want to see unicorns and mermaids. And it's got to be better than whatever lame camping vacation Mom and Dad are planning."

I stalked back to my room, miffed. Sure, it wasn't a thrilling story. It wasn't supposed to be. But it was set on the perfect vacation planet. And I'd got all the details right. I was sure of it.

CHAPTER TWO
UNICORN WORLD

Sunday. P.P. (Perfect Planet) Day. Maggie and I had agreed to meet by the tree fort at two in the afternoon. The night before, after she'd gone to bed, I'd snuck out to the garage and retrieved the circlet gizmo and the translator nets from under some boxes of Christmas ornaments (a safe spot, I'd figured, at least until December).

The squeaking bars of a hamster cage stopped me before I could leave my room. Leggy's no hamster—he's a sausage-shaped, six-legged little guy that snuck back to Earth with us after our last trip.

"Sorry, bud, I can't take you along," I explained to him. "You might get lost or something, and I don't want to spend my vacation searching all over for you. But we'll only seem to be gone for a few minutes. I'll even bring you a souvenir!" Then I fed him a stick of his favorite beef jerky and slipped out of the room.

Striking off through the woods, I carried the alien stuff in a backpack along with other supplies. Maggie and I had been totally unprepared for the last trip we'd taken. This time I'd packed flashlights, pocketknives, binoculars, granola bars, Band-Aids, and two translation devices— other pieces of outer-space technology that we'd brought back home. They helped us understand alien languages, and they looked like cafeteria hairnets. I'd thought it would be a good idea to bring cell phones until I realized there wouldn't be any cell towers or satellites. So I'd rummaged around in the garage and found my dad's old set of walkie-talkies. They were kind of bulky, but Maggie has a way of rushing off places, and I thought we shouldn't lose contact. Try explaining to your mom that you'd lost your kid sister on some weird beach planet.

When I got to the fort, Maggie was already there.

I sat down, opened my backpack, and handed Maggie a flashlight, a pocketknife, a walkie-talkie, and her translation hairnet. She slipped them in her own lumpy backpack, cramming the tools in between a striped scarf and some junk jewelry, and put the translator on her head. I wondered what else was in there. Probably bags of those gross gummy worms she liked. Then I pulled out the alien gizmo. It was actually pretty cool-looking: one part was a silver, crownlike circlet with three blue jewels. The other part was a high-tech staff-thing. Putting the crown and one of the translator nets on my head, I handed the staff to Maggie.

"Ready?" she said, grinning and waving the staff.

Suddenly I wanted to yell "No!" Scary memories from last time came rushing back. But I couldn't back out. During our first trip, Maggie got the idea that I was some sort of a hero. Like big brothers are supposed to be, I guess. Not a major wimp, like I really am. It was a kind of cool change.

I took a big breath and grabbed Maggie's hand: "Ready." I reached into my back pocket and looked over the finished draft of my story. I didn't want to mix up any details as I thought my way to the alien beach and wind up somewhere else. My head jiggled as she jammed the edge of the staff into the circlet on my head. The sounds of birdsongs and rustling leaves cut out. A moment later, I felt like I was being turned inside out like a sweatshirt, shaken violently, and then yanked outside in again.

Sound came back: the soft hiss of waves on sand. Sun shone warmly on my eyelids. Slowly, I raised them. White sand sparkled into the distance. The air smelled fresh and tangy. An ocean stretched to the horizon, a brilliant blue-green. I'd only been to the ocean once before, when we'd visited an uncle. The skies had been gray then and the water rough and cold. But the scene before me looked even better than one in any travel brochure. I'd done it!

Maggie let out a whoop and ran down the beach. Feeling mighty pleased with myself, I sauntered down after her. The last doubt shuffled to the back of my mind.

I should have made it stay front and center.

Skipping along the wet sand, Maggie laughed and threw rocks into the incoming waves. I looked down. Pretty pebbles dotted the beach. I'd said in my little story that a unicorn prince had been trying to collect more pretty rocks than anyone else. He stumbled into a hidden cave, where he found a mermaid princess with her tail caught between boulders. She'd given him the giant pearl she was wearing, and he'd freed her by prying the rocks away with his horn. Like Maggie said, a lame story, but it got us to the beach.

Maggie called out from the edge of the gently lapping waves. "OK, Josh. It's really nice here, but where are the mermaids? And the unicorns?"

"Hey, I only said the creatures lived on this planet. I didn't say where or how many. Just enjoy the beach. Maybe we'll see them later."

I enjoyed the beach, at least. I saw some really amazing seashells with points and spirals. And the beach rocks were even better than the stones my uncle and I had looked for. These rocks were clear, with swirls of red, purple, or gold. I started picking some up, then remembered that I'd thrown an old marble bag into my pack for collecting stuff. I rummaged around until I found it and then poured a handful of beach rocks into the bag.

"I just saw a mermaid maybe!" Maggie called. I looked up. Nothing broke the ocean's glassy surface.

"Maybe," I called as I reslung my pack and returned

to rock hunting. "It could be dolphins or whales or that sort of thing. I didn't mention all the creatures this planet might have, just the ones you wanted."

In fact, I realized, *I didn't mention a lot of stuff.* I'd said there were forests beyond the sand, and there were. But I hadn't said anything about the purplish mountains beyond the woods or the even taller mountains curving up the coast. One peak had a little wisp of smoke trailing out of it. *A volcano?* I wondered. *Cool.*

There were sounds, too, that I hadn't written about. A pack of something monkeylike gibbered in the forest. Cawing birds skimmed over the waves. Like seagulls— no, more like flying snakes with seagull beaks. And then there was the roar.

A huge, hate-filled roar.

I spun around to look at the forest. Something big, black, and shaggy was stalking out of the trees. It roared again, baring gleaming white fangs. Maggie and I ran toward each other, colliding in a terrified hug.

"Th . . . think . . . think of another story!" Maggie stammered. But I couldn't think of anything except those teeth and . . . oh no . . . the single white horn jutting out of the beast's forehead.

"Maggie," I said, "I think that's one of your unicorns."

I thought back in horror to my sketchy story: *The one-horned prince strolled into the cave on his four long legs.* I hadn't exactly said "unicorn." I definitely hadn't specified "dainty white horses with silly rainbow-colored manes," like Maggie's got all over her room. But all of a sudden I wished I had. This creature was about as dainty as a grizzly bear, and its snarling face looked more like a lion's than a horse's. All that black shaggy hair might have looked cute on a dog one-tenth of the beast's size, but no way I was petting this thing.

"A story!" Maggie wailed. "Think!"

Trying desperately to think of something, I shut my eyes. They popped open again when the advancing creature spoke and my translator kicked in.

"Hairless things! Treasure stealers! Get off this beach!" It roared again. Two fangs curved down from its mouth like a saber-toothed tiger's.

"Run!" Maggie tugged and I followed. She darted down into the waves and leapt onto a chain of big rocks that poked out of the water. The rocks were slippery with seaweed, and we scrambled like frantic frogs. Finally, we reached the last rock. Nothing but ocean stretched beyond it. Trapped.

"Maybe it hates water?" Maggie whimpered.

It sloshed through the surf and pounced from rock to rock until it landed on the stone next to ours.

"Maybe not," I murmured.

The beast's shaggy face split into a saber-toothed snarl.

"Where are your tails? Your stupid hair? *Where are my rocks?*"

I knew that our alien translation device let us understand local speech, but it still was a shock to hear this horror talking.

"Er . . . right . . . your rocks. Are all the rocks here yours?"

"This is my rock-hunting beach! Hand your rocks over!"

The creature leaned forward. A pearly white globe hung on a chain around its neck. Maggie gasped.

"Doofmelopalan!" I blurted. "You're a unicorn prince!"

His round red eyes gave a startled blink. "Huh! I am known among the tree creatures."

"Well, sure," I managed. "You freed a sea princess in exchange for that big pearl."

His eyes narrowed to slits. "Nobody knows that but me and fool princess."

Beside me, Maggie piped up. "We know lots of stuff, Prince Doof-whatever. Like we know you're the youngest prince, and you're always trying to collect more rocks to impress your parents."

I poked her. That didn't seem like a diplomatic thing to mention. It wasn't.

"Secrets!" the prince hissed. "You steal secrets too!" He flexed a set of knifelike claws and leapt onto our rock. I cringed as he pried the circlet off my head with his horn. "I take pretty crown-thing in trade."

The circlet now hung on the horn like someone had just played ringtoss with it. It looked really dumb.

"Hey!" Maggie yelled. "We need that! We didn't steal your secrets anyway. We're big-time magic workers. We have mystic ways to learn things. So give us back that crown, or we'll turn you into something even horribler than you are."

I kept poking Maggie, trying to shut her up. But she's always got to do the big drama thing.

"Horrible? I am prince! You scrawny hairless things! You are horrible. I can rip you to shreds! Have you thrown into deep pits!"

Maggie stood up and brandished the staff. "And we can turn you into a speckled aardvark! But give us the circlet, and we'll call it even."

"You're making everything worse," I hissed.

"Well, it can't get much worse than it is now."

Man, was she wrong.

CHAPTER THREE
MERMAIDS TOO

I looked around frantically. The tide was going out—more slimy rocks poked out of the water. *We could scramble farther out,* I thought, *but what good would it do?* The hairy fanged thing had cut off our way back. I knew that if I could calm down enough, I could think of a new story, but the beast still had the circlet. My mind raced: *What if we swam away? Maybe this oaf of a unicorn can't swim.*

I glanced back at the newly emerging rocks. Something else had crawled out onto one. Maggie saw me staring and looked too.

Her eyes narrowed. "Josh, you've done it again. Is *that* supposed to be a mermaid? Just what exactly did you write about that one?"

I shrugged. "I didn't say much. I just said she was half-human and half-fish. Everyone knows what a mermaid looks like."

Maggie snorted. "Oh really? Just like everyone knows what a unicorn looks like?"

I looked again at the creature on the rock. The thing was half-person and half-fish all right, but not the way a mermaid's supposed to be. The front was basically human—human arms, legs, and stomach. The back was all fishy. A fin ran between stretches of smooth scales. A thick fish tail hung down behind its legs. The whole creature, even the human side, was a sickly gray color, including its long seaweedlike hair. The face looked kind of humanish, except for its bulgy eyes and the wide mouth full of pointy teeth.

The mer-thing grinned, but not at me and Maggie. Prince Doof fluffed up behind us like an angry cat—an insanely big, one-horned cat. "Well, well, well, what luck!" The newcomer chuckled. "I got a huge scolding for losing the mystic pearl to one of the enemy. Now I can take it back."

"Is that your Princess Nwen-whatever?" Maggie whispered.

"Nwenlapulo," I said miserably.

"No way!" Doof snarled at the mer-thing. "I bargained for it. Fair and square!"

"You cheated! I had no choice. Give back the pearl."

"Make me!" he roared.

The mer-thing just giggled and flapped her tail into the water. "Well, that's easy enough. But I have a better idea. I'll take you and these odd runts for ransom."

"Humans!" Maggie noted. "We're called humans." No one paid attention.

Doof laughed at the princess: "Just try!"

Nwen splashed her tail again. A dozen gray heads popped up from the water surrounding us. They began moving in.

"Wait!" I cried. "We're not with him!"

Nwen chortled. "So? You're still valuable as hostages. Get them!"

With that, the weird mer-things swarmed toward us, throwing nets overhead. The nets clung like spiderwebs. In seconds, we were yanked off the rocks and into cold, salty, and very unbreathable water.

I admit, I panicked. Drowning always sounded like a ghastly way to die. Maggie and I were caught in the same net. Doof, yelling awful, partially translated insults, was wrapped in another. Sinking underwater, we all kicked frantically. Beneath the surface, the nets bulged out and filled with air like balloons. Oddly enough, they didn't let in water either—a thin layer of something kept us protected.

The sea people dragged us swiftly through the ocean. The sides of our air bubble were clear enough to see through. We passed reefs, underwater cliffs, and lots of fish. Some fish darted by in clouds of red, gold, and electric blue. Others were dark and scary looking. Something the size of a whale swam up and nosed at our bubble, staring inside with six hungry eyes. The sea people yelled at it, and with an annoyed glower, it turned and glided away.

Huddled beside me, Maggie shivered. "You and your stupid stories!"

"Me? It was *your* idea for me to write it!"

"Yeah, and you got it all wrong."

"Only because you wanted it in a hurry. I didn't have time for details. And anyway, I told you it was a stupid idea to try the gizmo again. We don't even have an owner's manual!"

"Shut up, babblers!" roared the black bulk bobbing in the next bubble. "You got special powers? Get us out of this. Now!"

Shivering and angry, I sulked. It was all so unfair! Unfair that Doof demanded we escape after snatching the only thing that made escape possible. Unfair that Maggie blamed me when it was all her fault. Was *I* maybe being a little unfair about the unicorns and mermaids? No! Well, maybe a little.

Beside me, my sister was quietly crying. My anger drained away. "Maggie—I'm sorry."

She sniffled. "I'm sorry too."

"We'll get out of this," I said, speaking more confidently than I felt. "I'll think hard about a story with us being back home. As soon as we can snatch the circlet back, we're out of here."

I could feel her nodding in the gloom beside me. "Sure. You can't have an adventure without a little danger. Right?"

"Right."

The water around us was getting lighter. *We must be coming closer to the surface,* I thought. I could see three sea people pulling our net. The rest were dragging

Doof. Even underwater, he must have weighed a ton.

I was hoping we'd be out in the sunlight soon. Nope. We did break the surface but in some sort of cave. A dome of rock covered the water, with sunlight filtering through a few random cracks. Our captors dragged us toward a rocky island and dropped the balloon nets. The sides fell away and we found ourselves sitting in shallow, cold water. Maggie and I squealed, Doof bellowed, and we all splashed our way to the island. Once on the dry rocks, Doof shook himself, spraying us with more water than the biggest, hairiest dog in the world could have.

Behind us, a mer-creature laughed. Nwen. "You land people are ridiculous. But ridiculous or not, you are my prize. You'll make up for all the trouble I got into for losing the pearl."

I watched her put the trinket back around her neck. To my horror, she was also wearing our alien circlet.

Nwen laughed again. "Well, off to talk with Mom and Dad! I'll finally get the praise I deserve. See you later, lo-o-osers."

"Not if I see you first," Maggie mumbled as the sea people splashed out of sight. "I definitely do not like that kind of mermaid."

Doof snarled. "All sea creatures are the same. Nasty cheats. Throw spiky, slimy things at us in battle. Not rocks like we use. They'll leave us to starve."

That last part didn't prove quite true. A little later, a couple of sea people wobbled out of the water carrying two baskets. "Don't eat it all at once," one laughed nastily. "Their Majesties take their time deciding things."

The mer-things looked odd standing on land, with their tails hanging down behind them. But when they dived back in the water, they were really graceful. Like swans that look goofy once they step out of a pond.

Maggie peered into one of the baskets they left behind. "Yuck, dead fish!"

Shiny, smelly dead fish. I know some fancy restaurants charge a lot for raw fish, but you couldn't pay me to eat them. "I guess this basket's for you," I told Doof as I went to look at the other one.

"Huh! Me, eat animals? What sort of brutes are you? Other basket is mine. Seaweed!"

Astonished, I stared again at his claws and fangs. "You're a vegetarian?"

He sniffed and rummaged in the basket. "All great creatures are." With that, he grabbed a rubbery bundle of seaweed and shredded it with his claws. He then stuffed what looked like a wad of green noodles into his huge mouth.

Fine, I thought. *Eat that nasty-looking stuff.* I peered back at the other basket. *But raw fish?* My stomach was grumbling. "Guess we'd better figure out a way to cook these things," I said to Maggie.

The matches I'd brought in my backpack were soaking wet, but I thought maybe I could start a fire with my binoculars—turning them around and focusing a sunbeam on some dry seaweed. It took forever. Doof watched us struggle with a smug smile on his face, chewing all the while.

I'd never cooked a fish before, but I knew you had to clean out the insides first. I took out my pocketknife and got to work. Majorly gross. We cooked chunks of fish on sticks. Well, burned them black, and even then they tasted fishy. I've never liked fish.

The glints of daylight drifting through cracks in the ceiling faded. Looking up, I saw the remaining traces of light wiggling, like the cracks were moving around. At first I thought my eyes were going funny. Then I realized they were glowworms or something. They didn't give off much light, but there was enough for us to find scraps of driftwood and prop up a rough shelter.

It was getting cold. Maggie and I curled up together like two lost puppies and listened to Doof snoring in the nest of dried seaweed he'd scraped together. *Snoring* doesn't capture it. He sounded like a jet plane with engine trouble. Still, I envied his wooly coat.

After a while, Maggie stopped shivering and fell asleep. I couldn't. I wished I wasn't the big brother who was supposed to be brave. I wished I could just wail in misery and suck my thumb. Well, not exactly, because my thumbs tasted of fish. But I was miserable.

Partway through the night, the snoring stopped. The sound of quiet tears replaced it. Could that fierce-looking hulk be feeling as miserable as I was? That was kind of strangely comforting. I eventually stopped thinking about what tomorrow would bring and slept.

Thinking about it wouldn't have done much good anyway. I could never have guessed the things we'd see next.

CHAPTER FOUR

WEIRDOS AND SLIMEBALLS

We woke to the sound of snide laughter. After a totally confused "where are we" moment, Maggie and I peered over our driftwood wall. Four sea people were climbing awkwardly out of the water, dragging a balloon net behind them. Princess Nwen was in the lead, our silver circlet glimmering on her head.

"Well, well. Look at you weirdos. What a pathetic little house you've built. And you, horn-face, your feeble nest is even worse." Doof glared at her from atop his pile of seaweed. "I brought you company. Maybe he's a better builder. He's certainly a talker."

One of her fellow sea people slashed open the new bubble net. Out tumbled a furious ball of curly orange hair. "I must protest!" it shrieked, jumping to its two

37

feet. The closest thing it looked like was a monkey. More than we humans looked like monkeys, anyway. Maybe a cross between a monkey, a poodle, and a pumpkin. Two tails. It wore what looked like a hunter's vest, camouflage green with lots of pockets.

"You cannot detain me!" it squawked. "I am royalty! I'm on a diplomatic mission!"

I groaned inside. More angry royalty. And I hadn't even mentioned creatures like these in my story.

Nwen flashed her sharky smile. "Yeah, right. Diplomatic. More like a spy mission. Well, you ought to

bring a nice little ransom. So shut up and wait for the king and queen to sort you out."

I jumped to my feet. "What about the two of us? We're not spies. We're not royalty. We're worth nothing to you."

"Yeah," Maggie chimed in. "No one's going to pay you for us. So, just give back that crown thing you stole from Doof and that Doof stole from us. Give it back and we'll be out of your hair . . . or weeds or whatever."

Doof charged toward Nwen from behind us. "And me! I'm a prince! Thieving slimeball!"

Nwen dodged his horn and slid back into the water. She resurfaced laughing, "Well, have fun together, misfits!"

"What a snot!" Maggie cried. "I'm sure glad she's not a real mermaid."

Doof sliced at the water with his horn. The fuzzy pumpkin-monkey grabbed up rocks and hurled them angrily into the water.

"What impudence!" the newcomer yelled. "I, Prince Igiwadi, cast into durance vile with these . . . these . . ."

He turned on us. "I recognize that grotesque brute. My kind has an ongoing skirmish with his kind. But what are you two?"

"We're humans," I answered. "And we don't belong here."

"I'd say you don't," he replied. "But my current predicament is *your* fault!"

"No way!" Maggie said. "We've never even seen you. Or *read* about you," she added, glowering at me. I shrugged.

The creature raised himself to his full height, which was about to Maggie's waist. "I am the Honorable Prince Igiwadi, youngest son of Their Magnificences King Ramalagani and Queen Ufapatoni, rulers of the forest."

Doof shambled up to us. "A little blowhard. My people rule the forest! His just scramble around in trees."

"You clumsy pointy-heads just grovel around in the dirt and dead leaves. We command the glorious heights, the soaring trunks, the heaven-reaching branches."

"Oh, stop fighting!" Maggie yelled. "We're all in the same mess."

Before they could snap at each other again, I asked the monkey, "What did you mean about being here because of us?"

He plunked down on a flat rock. "It is indeed all your fault! I was dutifully patrolling the forest edge, as is my custom, looking for heroic deeds to perform. I observed in the distance two figures shaped rather like my splendid people. They appeared to be marooned on a rock in the ocean. They and this annoying hornhead were abruptly abducted by a swarm of foul sea people. I raced through the trees in their wake, which eventually led me to the rocky island under which their putrid palace is known to rest."

I rolled my eyes at Maggie. She giggled. Well, at least this wordy guy was a change from Doof, who mostly grunted and cursed. The little orange guy hopped off his rock and began to pace, twisting and untwisting his two tails.

"From my vantage point on an arching palm, I spied still more aquatic fiends cavorting in the water near my shore. I hailed them, asserting that I was an ambassador from the glorious tree people, come to negotiate release of my two detained countrymen. When I ventured down to the shore, those slimy cheats treacherously captured me and, against my extensive objections, dragged me here."

Spinning around, he glared at Maggie and me. "And now I discover that all my heroics have been for naught!

For you two are shabby impostors, not noble tree creatures at all."

Doof snorted. "You're right about that. Impostors! Magic workers. Haw! Can't even magic us out of here!"

"That's because you stole our crown, you miserable phony unicorn!" Maggie shrieked. "And now that phony mermaid has it!"

"Oh shut up, everybody!" I shouted. "So we all don't like each other. Fine. But we're still stuck in this together. Maybe together we can figure some way to get out. Do either of you know what the mer-king and queen are likely to do to us?"

Everyone went silent. The fake unicorn and the pumpkin-monkey looked down at their feet.

Maggie broke in. "Come on, that annoying Nwen called us all hostages. Doesn't that mean they'll demand something valuable to get us . . . get you, anyway . . . back?"

To my astonishment, Prince Igi slumped to the ground and started sobbing. "Oh yes indeed," he blabbered through a curtain of tears, "since I am a prince, they will demand a grand ransom. Jewels and other treasures. And . . . and my parents won't give them anything!"

He crumpled up and sobbed some more.

After a stunned moment, Maggie knelt beside him and patted his curly orange back. "Oh, of course they will. You're their son. They'll want you back."

Igi looked up and sniffed. "No they won't. I'm the youngest prince. A failure at everything! That's why I pretended I was a diplomat. If you had been tree creatures and I had succeeded in liberating you, my parents would finally see that I was worth something."

He started sniffling again. I actually felt bad for the little guy. To my surprise, Doof apparently did too. Tears dribbled down the long black hair on his cheeks.

"So sad," he moaned. "Sounds like me."

"Does not," Igi sniffed. "You're a formidable presence! A hulking prince! The very forest trembles when you walk."

"Trembles?" Doof spat. "Ha! *I'm* the only one who trembles. I'm the runt of the royal family. Everyone makes fun of me. Won't play with me because I'm the youngest. A puny weakling!"

This behemoth, puny? I thought. *I'd hate to meet the rest of his family.*

"Why do you think I hang around that lousy beach?"

he continued miserably. "The others won't let me play in the good places. I keep hoping I'll find enough nice rocks to impress my parents. But never find enough to impress anyone! They won't trade a bucket of warm doo for me."

Both princes huddled on the rocky ground, crying up a storm. Maggie and I looked at each other. "At least we've got friends back home," Maggie said.

I nodded. "And parents who love us," I said. I instantly wished I hadn't. *Parents who don't know we're on a weird alien world. Parents who might miss us.*

Maggie and I were about to join the crying brigade when the water around us began to churn. Lots of sea-people heads popped up.

Nwen paddled closer, a sharky grin on her face. "Their Majesties will see you now. Ransoms will be arranged, and at last I'll be getting the notice I deserve."

I stared at our silver crown gleaming on her weedy head. Ransoms arranged for the others, maybe, but not for us. We had to get that circlet back!

CHAPTER FIVE
FEELING THE RUMBLE

Heroics were out. Before I could take even a few steps forward, mer-guards rose from the water and threw a net over us. All of us.

Maggie and I scrunched against Doof and Igi. The two princes thrashed so much I was afraid Doof's horn was going to skewer somebody. Maggie and I scrambled onto his furry back to get out of the way. Doof bellowed, and then we all tumbled in a heap as Nwen's guards dragged the net into the water.

Cramped together, we swished through the blue-green gloom. After a while, we popped into the air again. Not the open air, though. Another cave—a much larger one. Glowing green seaweed hung around everywhere like party streamers. But this didn't feel like a party.

Sea people were everywhere. Some floated lazily in the water; others lolled upon the many rock islands jutting above the water. They all turned and stared at our bubble net as it bobbed on the surface.

A guard pushed us like a beach ball toward the largest island. A stream of water flowed from the island's highest point and down its side. Two thrones had been carved right in the waterfall. Two very large, very ugly sea people sat in them.

"The king and queen of the mermaids should *not* look like that," Maggie muttered.

The guard leapt toward us, slashing our bubble net open with a spear. It collapsed, sending us stumbling into shallow water at the base of the king and queen's island. As we splashed, laughter echoed through the cavern. It didn't sound cheerful. And all the faces turned

toward us didn't look very cheerful either.

The one who must have been the king leaned forward. With his knotty green beard, he looked like he'd fallen facedown in a plate of spinach. After a moment, he shifted his fishy stare to Nwen.

"Well, insignificant youngest daughter, what have you brought us besides amusing oafs from the land?"

Nwen stood on the edge of the island. She looked less confident than before. Her head was lowered, and I even thought I saw her shaking. "I bring you treasures snatched from our enemies, noble father and mother. Two princes and a couple of rare freaks. They can all be traded for great ransoms."

Next, the queen leaned forward. I had to agree with Maggie. Her round fish eyes and pointy teeth did not make her look very mermaidy.

"If so, daughter, it is the first time you have brought us anything other than trouble."

Around the base of the island, a dozen young sea people clapped and giggled. *Nwen's brothers and sisters?* I guessed. *Not very nice ones.*

The king stroked his seaweedy beard. "Perhaps there is merit in this idea. Though since the days of the Parting, little good has come from our dealings with the land or tree creatures."

He leaned farther forward. "And less good has ever come from ventures of yours, youngest daughter. . . ."

Suddenly he pitched forward. So did the queen. Around them, spear-toting guards toppled like toy soldiers. Huddled on the ground already, we prisoners didn't fall over. But we felt the cave tremble around us.

"Earthquake!" Maggie gasped.

"Is it an earthquake if it's not on Earth?" I said stupidly.

Nwen had fallen only a few soldiers away from us. I plunged forward, my fingers only inches from the silver circlet, but a recovered guard grabbed me around the waist and hurled me back toward the other captives.

The ground continued to shake. Rumbling, shrieking, and splashing filled the air. Chunks of rock began falling from the ceiling, splashing into the water. A big wave sloshed onto the island, soaking us. Igi clung to Doof's furry side like an orange spider.

Finally, the earthquake (or whatever you call it) stopped with a last jolt. Everywhere, sea people rushed around like bugs under an overturned rock. Guards helped the king and queen back onto their thrones. Others struggled to their feet, herding us together again.

Maggie looked toward the thrones. She poked me.

"Looks like a family conference."

Nwen and a bunch of her brothers and sisters crowded around the king and the queen. Everyone was waving their hands and talking at once. I couldn't make out much of it. Not until the king jumped to his feet, pointed at Nwen, and bellowed, "Seize her!"

Guards jumped forward, wrapping Nwen with what looked like strands of seaweed. She screamed. Her brothers and sisters laughed. Just before the guards tossed Nwen among us, a guard ripped the silver circlet off her head and tossed it on the ground.

Maggie and I dove toward the gizmo, banging our heads together. Before I could say "ouch," the circlet was lost under scuffling feet, and we were wrapped in seaweed too. Doof put up a fight before they seaweed-wrapped him as well. But finally, he was bound tight as a fly in a spiderweb.

Guards stuffed us into another balloon and kicked it into the water. The next few minutes were miserable. Aching, bound like mummies, we drifted through gloomy

depths. Worse was the feeling that my last chance to return home might have been trampled by mer-feet.

You'd think that would be the worst moment of my life. You'd be wrong.

I was squashed up next to Nwen. I should have been really angry with the miserable little fish girl. But it's hard to be angry with someone who's crying like her heart's broken.

"So what's going to happen to us?" I managed to mumble through strands of seaweed.

Her sobbing trailed off into wet snuffles. "They're going to sacrifice us to Googoroo."

"What? Who?"

"The volcano god."

There. *That* was the worst moment of my life.

CHAPTER SIX

LIKE A BAD MOVIE

The long trip in the balloon net was as nasty as always. But I hardly noticed. I was focused on how the trip might end—with Maggie, myself, and our new companions dropped into a volcano. Nwen kept sobbing. Doof cursed. Igi whimpered.

"This can't be happening," Maggie muttered over and over again. "It's like some corny old movie script.

Sacrificed to the volcano god? It's too stupid. Even you couldn't write a story this stupid."

"I *didn't* write it. I just tuned into a world that had your stupid unicorns and mermaids in it."

"I am not stupid!" Nwen unexpectedly snuffled. "Just unlucky. Unlucky that I ever met any of you!"

Maggie started to snap back, but we needed information, not more arguing. "So *why* are we being thrown to this volcano god?" I asked. "We haven't done anything."

"The earthquake. The sea priests figure that Googoroo is angry that outsiders were brought into his realm."

"That's nuts!" Maggie complained. "And anyway, *you're* not an outsider. Why'd your parents throw you in with us?"

"Because *I* brought *you* in. And you brought the god's anger down on us."

"But your parents can't throw you into a volcano," I said. "You're their own child!"

Igi stopped wailing and joined in. "Where do you two ignorant misfits come from? She's obviously their *youngest* child. Youngest children are deemed worthless until they prove themselves. That is, prove that they are something other than a failure."

"That's what we all are," Doof brayed. "Youngest children. Failures! Doomed!"

All three began to cry. Maggie huddled even closer to me. "This world is totally crazy," she said. "Youngest kids are supposed to be the spoiled and pampered ones, right?"

"Always worked for you," I said. She glared at me. "Don't worry," I added. "We'll get out of this. There's got to be a way."

That's what I really hate about the big brother role. You've got to act all competent and cool. But really, I had no clue about how to fix things. And I was scared out of my mind.

It didn't help that the water around us was steadily getting warmer. Ahead, it took on a red glow, like in those nature films about volcanoes.

Finally, we popped to the surface next to a beach. And not a white-sand tourist-brochure beach. This beach was all chunks of black rock. Nothing grew—no trees, no grass. The rock bed sloped sharply up into a mountain. A mountain with smoke coming out the top and several glowing-red gashes down its side.

The sea people hauled us onto the beach, pried open

our net, and yanked us all out. They worked fast and kept looking over their shoulders at the smoking peak. Still wrapped like mummies, we were picked up, thrown over mer-shoulders, and carried up the mountainside. Well, the guards tossed Igi and me over their shoulders. Four of them were needed to carry Doof.

Although they took the three of us up the right slope of the volcano, the guards started to carry Maggie and Nwen up the left. "Hey, where are you taking my sister?" I yelled at the sea person whose shoulder I was bouncing upon.

"Fool," he replied. "She and the princess go to the female side. You and these others go to the male side. Googoroo won't eat his food mixed."

Right, I thought. As a very little kid, I didn't want anything on my plate to touch. Peas, potatoes, cheese— they all had to be in their separate piles. If they mixed together, I threw a tantrum. No way did I want to see a volcano's tantrum.

But then, if I was thrown into a crater of bubbling hot lava, I wouldn't be seeing anything for much longer.

CHAPTER SEVEN
NOT MUCH BETTER

After a long jaunt up, the guards threw us hard onto bare, rocky ground. The volcano's surface was hot, and it shuddered a little.

I was tied so tightly in seaweed that I couldn't move my head. On one side, I made out a faint red glow. On the other, I glimpsed the sea people scuttling away.

"Hey!" I yelled. "You can't leave us here!"

"Don't worry," one of them yelled back. "You won't have to wait long. Googoroo gets hungry in a hurry."

Doof roared, vowing to do horrible things to the fleeing guards. Lying beside me, Igi shrieked so loudly he nearly deafened me. But it did no good. Flopping like a seal, I tried to turn enough to look into the volcano crater. It wasn't the big main crater, I guessed, just a little dent in the mountain's side. But that didn't make the bubbling lava inside look any nicer.

And just two days earlier I'd been planning a perfectly safe trip to a tourist-brochure planet, packing my backpack, assuring myself nothing could go wrong this time.

My backpack! Had I packed anything useful? I squirmed, trying to wriggle my arms out of the bonds, but I only strained an elbow. The more I thrashed, the more I bumped against Igi, and the more noise he made.

"Will you pipe down!?" I yelled. "Look, do you want to be useful? Do you want to get out of here?"

Finally, his shrieking stopped. "Yes," he whimpered.

"All right," I said. Doof had stopped cursing, but I still had to shout over the lava pit's gurgling. "I'm wearing a pouch on my back. I can't reach it, but if you can wiggle a hand free and open it, there may be something in there that can help us."

I expected a long-winded complaint, but all he said was, "I am unable to move my hands extensively, but one of my tails is free." Something like a furry snake brushed the back of my neck. I suppressed a shiver.

"Right, now see if you can pull open the zipper."

I guess I hadn't realized that a talking two-tailed monkey from a strange planet might not have seen a zipper before. It took a while to explain how to work it, and then he had lots of fun just pulling it back and forth.

"Just leave it open. See if you can feel around inside and find my pocketknife."

Then I had to explain what a pocketknife was like. It took ages, but finally he pulled it out. I didn't trust him to cut me free without slicing up a lot more than seaweed. So I flopped around until I could get my fingers around the knife and pry it open. Once I'd sawed myself and Igi loose, I turned to Doof. But as soon as I'd freed his head, he used his horn to slash away the rest of the weeds.

Just then, the rock ledge under us heaved and cracked. We leapt away as the ledge split off and toppled into the boiling lava. It landed in a fountain of sparks.

"We must remove ourselves immediately!" Igi squeaked.

"Yeah, but where to?" I panted.

"There!" Doof pointed. On the inland side of the volcano's base, a ridge of black rock trailed off. Eventually it disappeared into shrubs and green forest.

"OK. But we've got to find Maggie first." I rummaged around in my backpack until I pulled out the walkie-talkie. I tried calling Maggie, though I knew it wouldn't do any good if she was still tied up. But she answered right away.

"You got to your pocketknife too?" I asked happily.

"Didn't need it. Nwen here has sharp teeth."

"Doof thinks we should head inland, to where the trees . . ."

The ground heaved like a sick dog. Maggie screamed into the walkie-talkie. I heard silence, then, "We're okay. The rock we were just on fell into the volcano. Let's go!"

"Right. Over and out. Or whatever."

I turned to Doof and Igi to find them staring at me like I'd sprouted a halo or something. "Y . . . you . . . you *are* a magic worker," Doof stammered.

"Nah, we don't do magic," I began, then thought

better of it: *Being thought a magician might come in handy sometime.* "Well, only magic with some things. Now we've got to leave before the volcano god decides he wants another snack."

But it was hard to hurry. Small, sharp black rocks coated the ground. They clanked and crunched as we walked. I could feel them slicing up the soles of my running shoes. Igi squealed and hopped about so much that I ended up having to carry him. From his perch on my shoulders, he kept up a steady patter of detailed instructions about where to put my feet. I generally ignored him.

Harder to ignore was Doof, who didn't seem bothered by volcanic rock. He kept snapping at me to go faster, but the extra weight I carried made that hard.

As Doof and I argued, another quake shivered down the mountain ridge. It sent us tumbling painfully over the sharp black stones. Doof scrambled to his feet and yelled, "No more! Not poking along with weaklings! Not when the volcano can blow any minute!"

With that he galloped off, spewing black gravel behind him.

"So? Who needs you, you impetuous horn-head?"

Igi shrieked from my shoulders. "Some fine example of nobility you present!"

Watching him go, I felt a little emptier. Doof was hardly a friend, but at least he was somebody I knew on this strange, scary planet.

I called Maggie again on the walkie-talkie. She and Nwen were all right but making slow progress. We agreed to meet up at a sliver of black rock we could both see on the far side of the volcano.

Igi and I had nearly reached the landmark when aftershocks from the quake swept under us. It was like being hit by a tennis racket, with us as the balls. Igi shot off me as I catapulted backwards. Ahead of us, the sliver of rock cracked, shot partway into the air, and then plunged into the ground a few feet from my head.

Above us, glowing red cinders floated down like Fourth of July fireworks. I staggered to my feet, turned to run, and smashed into something black and hairy.

"OK! You win. Even a youngest prince has got to do noble stuff," Doof grumbled. "Climb on my back! Both of you!"

We grabbed handfuls of shaggy black hair and pulled ourselves up. "Wait!" I cried. "We can't leave without Maggie."

"So let's leave!" Maggie called as she stumbled toward us. She was almost carrying Nwen. I guess the sea princess's webbed feet weren't made for running over volcanic rock.

"I can't carry two more!" Doof protested.

I reluctantly slid off his back and boosted Nwen onto it. At least Maggie and I had shoes on.

Then we all ran.

The volcano behind us sounded like a giant with indigestion. Occasional cannon blasts sent huge boulders flying through the air. The ground would lie still for a moment, then start bucking again.

We reached a stretch where scrubby plants began to appear among the bare rocks. Doof stumbled to a stop, and Maggie and I collapsed beside him. "Should be safe soon," Doof gasped. "Googoroo does this a lot. Usually doesn't kill stuff this far away."

Behind us, the sun was setting amidst a swirl of pink clouds. Patches of orange glowed like angry eyes on the face of the volcano. It was a scary view, but after what we'd been through, I almost felt safe. The feeling didn't last long.

CHAPTER EIGHT

DANGER FROM ABOVE

Against the smoky pink sky, black spots zoomed toward us. *More rocks shot from the volcano?* I wondered. *No, not unless some rocks here have wings.*

They were birds. A whole squadron of big birds, headed directly toward us.

"Nooooo!" Igi wailed.

"What are they?" Maggie and I both asked.

"Zurz," Doof snarled. "Evil zurz. Eviler than tree creatures. Eviler than sea creatures. Evil sky creatures. Now we really gotta run!"

Soon we were surrounded by flapping purple wings. Claws dug into my shoulders and yanked me off the ground.

Everything was a blur—wings, noise, and pain. Then I was given a really cool aerial view of the nearby volcano. Cool, except that I was dangling right over it from the claws of a big bird. I crossed my fingers and hoped he had a good grip.

The flock flew past the volcano and on into the darkening night. My shoulders throbbed with pain, and my head buzzed with questions. *Is this a rescue or an abduction?* I wondered. *What other horrible surprises could this perfect vacation spot hold?* With no answers coming, I just hung limp and watched the view.

We were closing in on a range of white peaks. The snow on top glowed in the moonlight. Or *moons'* light. I could see at least five moons in the sky. That was a surprise. My little story hadn't been set at night, and the night before we'd been stuck in that watery cave.

The birds were silent except for the steady flapping of their wings. Even Igi's complaining and Doof's cursing died down as we neared what looked like a giant nest on a high mountain peak.

Swooping low, the birds let us loose. I landed with a thud in a giant upturned mattress of sticks and grass. The others thudded down around me. Doof began cursing again. My translator didn't give me all the details. I just knew that if I had used anything like those words at home, I would have been in serious trouble.

Our captors and a bunch more like them stood around looking at us. This was the first good look I'd gotten at these zurz. Weird—but what else could you expect on this planet?

They were big as a grown man, with flat, round-eyed faces, sort of like owls. Only they seemed to be covered with purple scales, not feathers. Halfway along their wings, hands stuck out, sort of like on bats. And their beaks looked really, really sharp. So did the teeth inside them.

The largest of the zurz hopped forward. "Welcome to the Feast of the Hatchlings!" it croaked.

A feast. That sounded good. We hadn't eaten in ages.

I looked hopefully around but didn't see any food. My stomach growled. Maybe we *were* the food.

Behind the big zurz were rows of little zurz. They began clacking their sharp little beaks and chanting "Food! Food! Food!"

"Soon, little ones, soon," the adult zurz replied.

Igi waved his palms in the air. "Wait! I have heard the stories about you vile creatures. I am familiar with the rules. Feast of the Hatchlings. A three-day ceremony. But you are not permitted to eat the first day's offerings if those offerings have something better to offer."

The big zurz snorted. "What offerings could a mismatched lot like you have for us?"

"Oh, countless treasures!" Igi looked around our little group. "I'm certain that we all possess great treasures. Correct?"

Doof stood up, shaking bits of straw out of his fur. "Got rocks. Pretty rocks." He reached one paw into his fur, fumbled around, and pulled out my old marble bag. He spilled a stream of beach rocks onto the nest floor.

The adult zurz all leaned over and stared at the offering. Then the leader laughed. "Rocks! We can pick up rocks anywhere we wish. But that's fine. Even by yourself, you will make a fine big meal."

With a moan, Doof sank down again, a sad, defeated look in his beady red eyes.

I stood up. "Then let me make his offering for him." From my backpack, I pulled out a flashlight—and gave up on doing any late-night reading during the trip. "Behold," I boomed. Or tried to boom. It might've sounded more like a croak. I flicked the flashlight on and off, shining its light across the flock. The zurz were stunned.

"The sun's light from a stick!" the head bird said. "The horn-head can skip the first feast."

The crowd of little zurz squeaked in protest until glares from the adults silenced them.

"Now, you, sea person. Have you something to offer?"

As he pointed a wing toward her, Nwen hid her face in her webbed hands. "Nothing. Well, I had the mystic pearl, a family treasure, but mother took it back. . . ."

Maggie seized the moment: "Bah, pearls are nothing! I will make her offering—something you have never seen on this world. Sacred statues of mythical beasts from our world of power and magic!" Dramatically, she unslung her backpack and pulled out two toys: a plastic unicorn with a rainbow tail and mane and a jointed

plastic mermaid with multicolored sequin fish scales.

The head zurz snorted. "Huh. What would we possibly..."

Squeaking, a young zurz wriggled past him. "I want, Da-da! Get them, get them, please!"

The father scowled. "Hush, Zoofoo! What a foolish princess you make. None of the others make such embarrassing sights of themselves!" The little one looked up with big, tear-filled eyes. The adult grumbled. "All right, all right. Sea person skips the first feast too."

Then he glared directly at Maggie. "But you, weird freaky creature. You just bought a pass for the sea girl only. What about yourself?"

"No problem," Maggie said with a theatrical bow. Amazing how Maggie can be a drama nerd even when something is planning to eat her. "I have here jewels from our mystical land. Jewels of great beauty and untold worth!"

Good thing the worth was untold, because Maggie held a handful of cheap plastic beads from birthday parties, Mardi Gras parades, and Halloween costumes. But on a world with no plastic, they did look pretty special.

Half the adult zurz whistled and fluttered forward. Their leader had to shoo them back. "Another pass," he growled. Then he turned to me.

I was ready. "Sir, you, I see, are a great leader. For your kind, eyesight must be important. But is your eyesight truly the best? It can be, with *this*!" I took out the binoculars and handed them to him, hoping the focus was right. "Hold them to your eyes and see farther than anyone else."

He fumbled with them a bit and then let out a delighted squawk. "Amazing! Another pass." Sighing, the big bird looked at Igi. "And you, tree vermin, this was your idea. I suppose you have a treasure hidden about you as well?"

The little guy hopped up and began capering about. "Oh indeed, a great treasure. Observe: a royal crown!"

He reached into his vest and pulled out a silver crown with blue jewels. Our alien circlet! Our ticket home! The little thief must have snatched it up in all the confusion back at the sea palace. And now he was going to give it to this scaly purple owl-thing!

CHAPTER NINE

SHAKY PLANS

Maggie shook her head *no* wildly. I dove for the circlet, plucking it out of Igi's hands and stuffing it in my jeans pocket. The scaly owl king barked a protest.

"You wouldn't want that piece of trash, Your Greatness," Maggie said. "It's just a cheap costume piece. Now, I have something that you'll *really* like. Something worth way more than this little orange fellow's life." She reached again into her backpack. *How much weird stuff did she pack?* I wondered.

She pulled out a mirror. Its plastic handle was fake gold, and on its back was a sticker of a character from some movie she loves to watch. A great white owl!

The reaction was amazing. All the zurz, big and little, howled and dropped to the ground. Their leader grabbed the mirror with a trembling wing-hand. "An image of the great god Oofoofur! And a reflecting scepter! You are indeed all passed from the first feast."

The little guys squealed in disappointment until the lead guy snapped, "Silence! Tomorrow's feast will be all the tastier for waiting." Then the crowd lifted off in a flurry of clattering wings.

We were alone in the big nest. I walked to the edge and peered over. A steep, slippery-looking cliff dropped hundreds of feet into a dark valley. Not the sort of place you could get away from without wings. I trudged back to the center and slumped down.

"What now, hairless ones?" Doof grunted. Then he looked at me. "Eh . . . thanks for saving me with that light-stick."

"Sure," I mumbled. Hearing Doof sound humble was even weirder than hearing him roar.

Igi reached toward me. "I must extend my gratitude as well. Now please return to me that silver crown. I found it, and I find it extremely attractive."

"And it's ours!" I replied. "We need it." The little guy looked like I'd stolen his best friend. "Okay, maybe I'll give you something else in trade. Maggie, got anything else in that bag of yours? Why did you bring all that junk anyway?"

She smiled her infuriating I-know-better-than-you smile. "I planned to give them as gifts to the mermaids and unicorns here—if they'd been proper mermaids and unicorns." She rummaged in her backpack some more. "How about this?" She pulled out a gold plastic medallion that hung from a wide red ribbon. It had come from a school field day.

Igi's sad eyes switched to happy. "Stupendous!"

I hung it around his neck. "Just keep it hidden in your fur, or our hosts will want it too. Now Igi, you seem to know a lot about these guys. Can we keep getting out of being eaten by giving them junk? Maybe we've got enough for another round or two."

He gave a sad shrug. "Not according to the stories. The second day of the ceremony is supposedly devoted to entertainment.   Dancing, singing, reciting. The proposed 'food' only escapes being eaten if it can out-entertain the zurz."

I looked around at our little group, huddled together in the giant bird nest. "Any of you guys good dancers?" Silence. "Singers?" More silence.

"*I* can sing!" Maggie protested.

"No you can't. Not if your life depended on it. Which it does."

She stepped closer and whispered to me. "Maybe it doesn't. We have the circlet now."

"Yeah, I know, but . . ." I gestured to the miserable-looking group. Maybe those three weren't the nicest creatures in the universe, but we'd been through a lot together in the last day. "We can't just leave them to be eaten."

Maggie nodded. "Right. But even if you put on the circlet and think us back home, we can't take them with us. They'd be freaks! They'd end up in a zoo or a circus."

I shook my head. "I know. But I'm getting kind of a crazy idea."

I walked over to Igi, who was curled up in a ball, half-asleep. "You mentioned that 'reciting' was one of the entertainments. Do you tell stories here?"

He blinked at me. "Stories?"

Maggie butted in. "You know, made-up adventures. Fiction."

He blinked again. "What we recite isn't made-up. How could it be? We all tell the tales about the Beginnings— when all the peoples of the world lived together. And then how they quarreled, warred, and came to live apart."

Doof lumbered over to join us. Nwen stopped patting her dry skin with snow and started listening too.

"Okay," I said. "Where we come from we have something called fiction. We take bits of real stuff and put them together into something a little different. Maybe if you guys tell me your tales about the Beginnings and all, I can recite something that will be entertaining enough to keep us from being eaten. But make sure you describe places that really exist on your world."

They all looked a little confused. A frown crinkled Nwen's fishy face. "How could we describe something that *doesn't* exist? You people make no sense."

"Never mind that. Just tell me your planet's tales.

Who wants to start?"

Igi volunteered to go first. We all huddled together for warmth and listened to his long, wordy story. Then Nwen went and, finally, Doof. They all told basically the same story, but each one had some different parts too. They all argued loudly about those bits, but at least each version described one place the same way: the island where folks called the rock people lived.

While the other three argued about how many sons the first king of the horned land creatures had, Maggie sat beside me, fingering the alien staff she'd pulled from her pack. I knew what she was thinking—I'd been thinking about it too.

"Are you sure your plan is going to work?" she said quietly.

I wanted to say no, that I was totally unsure, and I didn't have much of a plan anyway. But I tried for the protective big brother thing. "Yes. Well, kind of. But I sort of think we've got to try it. Don't you?"

She looked over at the "mermaid," the "unicorn," and the little orange monkey. "Yeah. I mean, we could probably get ourselves home right now since we've got the staff and the circlet. But I keep thinking how I'd feel if we just skipped out and left these guys to get eaten. I mean, they aren't just some characters in a story. They're *real*. This whole world is real, even if it's really, really weird."

I nodded. Then the world got a bit weirder.

Maggie moved to put the staff away and squeaked. One of the little zurz was curled up beside her backpack. At Maggie's cry, it opened its big eyes. "Tell me about your magical world," it peeped. "Don't like this one much. Everyone's mean to me. So mean!"

It clutched Maggie's toy unicorn and mermaid in its wing-hands. I tried to remember what the head zurz had called this one. Something funny. *Foofoo? Googoo? No. Zoofoo.* "Hey, Zoofoo, why should we tell you stories if you just want to eat us tomorrow?"

She lifted up the toys. "Want to hear about place these from. Stupid brothers and sisters just want to eat." She hung her head. "I know I'm a bad princess. Bad princess."

I looked down at the little purple thing. Her scales looked almost like feathers when they weren't clattering around. "Don't tell me," I said, "you're the youngest too."

"Won't tell you if you don't want. But I am."

"What is the matter with this world?" Maggie snapped. "Why is the youngest kid always dumped on?"

By now the other three had stopped arguing and joined us. "That is the way it has always been," Igi said with a shrug. "From time immemorial."

"Yeah. It stinks," Doof added.

Nwen snorted. "Sure does."

Maggie stood up, hands on her hips. "Well, that's not the way it is on my world. I mean, Josh here is sometimes a pain, but I don't let him boss me around. And I'm the youngest. Why don't you guys revolt or something? Fight for youngest kids' rights!"

There we were, in danger of being eaten on a really awful planet, and my kid sister was trying to start a revolution. I grinned. *If Maggie wasn't such a pain, I thought, I could be really proud of her.*

I stood up too. "OK. Let's not get too crazy. I've got a plan that could maybe get us out of here. But you've all got to help." I looked down at the scaly owl-bat princess. "You want to help too, Zoofoo?"

She jumped up and down so much that her scales clattered like wind chimes. "Go to your world?"

I shook my head. "I don't think that would work. And you're safe here. No one's going to eat *you*."

"Want to go anyway!" A little zurz could be as stubborn as a human kid sister.

"Let's just work out the plan first."

We plotted until none of us could keep our eyes open any longer. The five moons had moved across the sky. While a sixth one was starting to rise, we curled up in a large, lumpy ball and fell asleep.

Well, the others fell asleep. I was too worried about my plan. What if it didn't work? What if these folks who had faith in me ended up getting eaten? What if I couldn't even get Maggie and me home, and we got eaten too?

I really hated being a big brother.

CHAPTER TEN

STORYTELLERS

You know how when you first wake up, there's a time when you're still warm and dreamy and the real day ahead of you hasn't butted in yet? I had that feeling. Warm sun on my closed eyelids, a warm, furry blanket beside me. *Furry?* Bam! Reality butted right in.

I shot upright. To my left, a mangy black behemoth was snoring loudly. To my right, my sister was curled up with a scaly, purply owlish thing, and next to them a fish person and a curly orange pumpkin-monkey were playing some sort of game with pebbles and straws.

I winced and prepared to face what could be a really bad day.

It started out, of course, with practically no breakfast. We all finished up the last of the granola bars from our packs, but dropping a granola bar into Doof's mouth was like dropping a pebble into an ocean. Stomachs grumbling, we rehearsed and set up for what seemed to me more and more like a really stupid plan. At least I didn't have much time to worry. Around midday we heard a sound like a giant silverware drawer being overturned in the sky. The zurz were coming.

The sky filled with many more than we'd seen the night before. With a chorus of squawks they landed, shoving into places around the outside of the giant nest. The littlest ones pushed to the front. They all looked eager—and hungry. Zoofoo slipped over to join them so they wouldn't know she'd spent the night with us.

The lead zurz trotted over to our huddled group.

"Welcome," he boomed. "Welcome to the second day of the Feast of the Hatchlings. Entertainment comes first. Then feasting. You, of course, are tasked to provide at least one." He grinned toothily. Then he spun around and spread both wings. "Let the entertaining begin!"

With that, all the adult zurz leapt into the air and began a crazy, noisy ballet above our heads. The little ones, squealing like teakettles, zipped in and out between the big guys, twisting, diving, and looping. I expected massive air crashes, but everyone seemed to be having fun. Except those of us on the ground waiting to be eaten.

After a final earsplitting yodel, they landed. The leader opened his beak. Sunlight glinted on his dagger-sharp teeth. "Your turn, honored guests. Or do you wish to concede and go directly to the feasting?"

The crowd of little zurz giggled nastily. I jumped up and shouted, "No, not at all. Your terrific air dance deserves some entertainment in return. We will now enact this world's great story!"

I walked to the center of the giant nest, feeling like a Roman gladiator thrown to the lions. I was wearing the silver circlet and Maggie's last pieces of costume jewelry.

STORYTELLERS 9|

She danced around me, waving the staff like a magic wand. Then she skipped back to join the others.

"In the beginning," I intoned, "this world was empty. Empty except for the Wind." At this, our little troupe of actors began whistling like raging wind. We had hidden one of our walkie-talkies at the far end of our stage, and the sound of even more wind roared from where nobody seemed to be. Our audience muttered in amazement.

I continued. "Wind was lonely. It dove down toward the ground, looking for friends." Our actors made rumbling noises like they were digging into dirt.

"Wind brought rocks up to the surface to be its companions. Wind made them a special place with mountains and caves to live in while it playfully blew around them." Our crew had pulled on grass nets we'd filled with rocks earlier that morning. They lumbered around, grunting and snorting. Doof was particularly good at the snorting.

"But Wind found the rocks to be too slow to play with. It began to weep with loneliness, and its tears filled up the big holes in the earth where the rocks had come from." The actors pretended to weep.

"Wind's tears became oceans. The Wind thought that

there might be friends in the water, so it dove down"—we made spitty, splashy noises—"and brought up creatures from the water." At this, Nwen threw aside her rock cape and began dancing around in her awkward fishy way. But the song she sang was pretty good. It sounded only a little like a stopped-up drain.

"The sea people had many sons and daughters, and they all treated each other equally." Maggie insisted I add that part. "But the sea people liked to live in the oceans, and the oceans were too wet for Wind. Wind was lonely again. It thought that if it made plants grow on the ground, other creatures might come to live there. So it blew dust into the air"—much dancing and throwing dirt about—"and the dust became the seeds of trees, grass, and flowers.

"Land creatures appeared and galloped about the land," which Doof did, with lots of snorting and bellowing. "They had many sons and daughters, and all treated each other like equals. But these people were too heavy for Wind to play with. Wind blew angrily against the orange flowers growing at the tops of trees, and the flowers' tops became tree creatures. The tree creatures loved to play in the treetops near to where Wind lived."

Igi leapt up and began cartwheeling around the nest, singing songs that sounded like a mouse being tortured. "Of course, they too had many sons and daughters, and all treated each other equally.

"But the tree creatures were so happy playing in the trees that they didn't have time to play with Wind. Finally, Wind blew fallen leaves into the air until they became creatures that played in the sky." At this, little Zoofoo soared into the air from where she had hidden. The audience gasped in surprise as she spiraled above them.

"The sky creatures had many sons and daughters who, of course, all treated each other equally. But they had so much fun flying in the sky that they too had little time for Wind. Wind became so angry with all the creatures that it created a terrible storm." Doof growled and stomped his feet near one of the walkie-talkies. Across the nest, the other walkie-talkie added to the noise. The whole audience shrieked and threw themselves flat on the ground. *Yes!* I thought. *Now here comes the tricky part.*

When the zurz sat up again, I cleared my throat. "All of the peoples cried out in fear. They asked Wind what could be done to make it happy. And Wind said . . .”

Maggie, hidden behind the others, got on a walkie-talkie and cried, “Friends! I need friends. Each of you creatures, choose one of your own! I will take them to my special island, and we will all talk about friendship.”

I continued. “Well, the peoples couldn’t decide who to send. In the end, each chose to send their ruler’s oldest child. Wind carried the eldest prince or princess from the sea, land, trees, and sky to the Island of the Wind. Then it swirled underground and brought up the eldest rock prince too. The island was beautiful and wild. From each corner, tall crystal peaks rose for Wind to swirl itself around. Between the peaks stood arches of rock and twisted trees for Wind to dance through. In the island’s center laid a deep pool of bluest water for Wind to splash in. And below the ground, rocky caves made perfect places for Wind to howl through. The rock, sea, land, tree, and sky children wandered around amazed.”

Maggie and the others slithered, galloped, and flew about, trying to look amazed. They looked pretty goofy, but the zurz seemed impressed. I guess they’d never seen a play before.

The others finally ended up beside me. I continued: "When the creatures came together, they began to argue about who was greatest. Rock angrily smashed against the sea princess, who slapped the land prince, who poked the tree prince, who spat on the sky princess. They fought and fought until Wind became so angry that it cursed them all. 'Go back to your separate lands,' it yelled. 'There you can hate and fight each other forever. Or until you send another delegation. Perhaps your youngest children this time," another Maggie addition, "creatures who can still learn about friendship. Then we shall see what we shall see."

All of us joined hands and slowly danced in a circle. With the others humming in the background, I chanted:

Your hate is so great.
Your plight is to fight.
In the end, you need friends.
Your youngest, do you send.

Okay, so it's lousy poetry, but it had a job to do. And the toughest part was next. I took a deep breath and chanted:

On the island's corners, crystal peaks rise,
glowing like rubies in the sunset skies.
Between them, stone arches stretch in a wall,
among gnarly old trees, twisted and tall.
In the island's center, a deep blue pool
lies in white sand like a precious jewel.
And there the Wind waits, longing for a friend.
Only there will this story happily end!

At the word *end*, Maggie jammed the staff into the silver circlet on my head. All sound cut out. It felt like we were shooting up, dropping down, and swirling sideways all at the same time.

We thumped to a stop. I opened my eyes, jumped up, and yelled. "We've done it! Look—the Island of the Wind! Crystal peaks, arched rocks, a blue pool, and . . ."

That's as far as I got before the ground wobbled and gave way under us. *Why*, I wondered as I fell into darkness, *do plans never go as planned*?

CHAPTER ELEVEN

A ROCKY PROBLEM

"Is everyone okay?" My voice trembled in the darkness, not sounding very fearless-leader-like. The rest of the gang groaned and grunted, but nobody seemed to have broken any bones.

I looked around. We'd fallen into something soft—the reason we weren't all smashed, I figured. The stuff on the ground was white and grainy, almost like sugar. And it glowed faintly. By its light, I looked at the startled faces around me.

"Missed some important details again?" Maggie said dryly.

"Hey, it's not *my* fault. We knew there were caves on the Island of the Wind because that's where the rock people were supposed to live. We couldn't have known the surface was thin enough that an umpteen-hundred-pound unicorn would send us through."

I turned to Doof. The glowing white sand sparkling all over his coat made him look a little more like Maggie's idea of a unicorn. He snorted. "Not *my* fault their caves are flimsy."

"Well, you might have tried to be light on your feet for once," Nwen snapped.

"Snatched off a mountaintop and dropped into this inhospitable cavern," Igi grumbled. "Hardly a major improvement."

"Okay, so this is pretty awful," Maggie said "But you're not on that mountaintop being eaten."

With a *whoosh*, little Zoofoo flew out of the mounded sand. "Awful? This wonderful, wonderful! Exciting new place!"

"So get your excited self up there," Nwen said, spitting sand out of her mouth, "and see if you can find us a way out of this place."

"Yes, yes! I'll spy out an escape route! Fun, fun!"

I was glad *somebody* seemed happy. I stood up and brushed at the powdery sand clinging all over me. Suddenly Maggie screamed.

I spun around. Squinting into the cave's darkness, I tried to see what new horrible thing was coming at us. Maggie shook at my arm.

"The circlet and staff! You were wearing them! Now you aren't!"

I slapped my forehead. Nothing there. "They must have fallen into the sand somewhere. Everybody look!"

Everybody dropped down and scooped at the sand. Everyone except little Zoofoo, who dutifully flew about looking for an exit. It was she who screamed next.

"Eeeek! Look over there!"

A rumbling, bouncing, cracking sound crept through the darkness. Lumpy shapes lumbered toward us.

"Rock people!" Nwen, Doof, and Igi screamed together.

"Surface creatures!" came the rumbling reply. "Get them! Squash them flat!"

That was our cue to run. Anywhere! But it's not

easy to sprint through sand. We floundered on, the glowing sand giving off just enough light to keep us from running into rock walls. The area's underground passages branched off like in a maze. Raucous cries of "crush" and "kill" followed behind us.

In front of me, Doof bellowed, and then I heard an enormous splash. The rest of us began to scream with him as we toppled into some sort of underground lake.

"I can't swim!" Doof burbled.

Nwen splashed her tail angrily. "Well, you don't have to, you oaf. It's shallow enough for you to touch the bottom. All of you, follow me!"

Maggie and I had taken swimming lessons in the hopes of someday going someplace fun enough to swim at. Someplace *not* like this. Igi flailed around in the water. He didn't sink, but he didn't make much progress either. Finally, he splashed toward Doof and climbed onto his shaggy black head, clinging to the horn like a soggy orange flag.

Nwen swam ahead of us, flapping her tail. There was enough glowing white sand on the bottom of the pool to keep us from being totally in the dark, but we mostly followed the sound of Nwen's splashes.

The rock people's grumbles seemed more distant after a few minutes. Maybe we were outpacing them. Soon we could see more light ahead, faint outdoorsy light shining through a large crack in the rock.

"Zoofoo!" I called. "Can we climb out that way?"

No answer. "Zoofoo!" My voice echoed through the cave. *She must have flown off when the rock people showed up,* I thought. I couldn't blame her, but I still felt kind of miffed. A rushing, roaring water sound interrupted my griping.

"Stop! Turn back!" Nwen yelled from up ahead. "Waterfall!"

I splashed and kicked, but a strong current pulled me forward. Maggie too. Together we smashed into Doof, who was trying to stand firm on the floor of the pool. The collision knocked him and his monkey passenger loose. All of us hurtled closer to the waterfall.

The sound of our screams was almost lost in the roar of water as we went over the edge. We landed with a massive splash, mostly made by Doof. Coughing, we floundered to the edge of what turned out to be a much smaller pool and dragged ourselves out.

"Water! Hate water!" Doof said, spitting a stream of

the stuff at Nwen.

"Well, it helped you escape the rock people, didn't it?" she spluttered. "We left those gravelheads far behind."

Looking up, I noticed a ring of boulders surrounding us. Boulders with eyes.

"Maybe not," I sighed.

CHAPTER TWELVE
GONE WITH THE WIND

The boulders had mouths too, sneering mouths. "You can't escape rocks where rocks rule," one laughed. A bunch of rock-bullies rumbled forward, grabbed us, and dragged us after them. These guys looked like they were made of randomly piled-up stones—several arms and legs apiece, one or two heads. Their pincer hands poked us as we moved. I could feel bruises blooming already.

Our painful trek ended in a high, rough-walled cave. Dozens of rock people squatted on boulders around us.

One of the creatures scrambled down from a high boulder. Some smaller rock people followed, looking like a mini-avalanche.

"Invaders from the surface!" the big one barked. "Enemies all. Crush them, bash them, smash them!"

"You can't do that!" Maggie screamed to be heard over the rocky cheers that erupted. "Two of us aren't even from your world! What did we ever do to you anyway?"

"You are different, ugly. You live weird places. You don't belong here!"

"So let us go!" I yelled. "Let us go back where we belong." I hoped I sounded brave and leaderlike, but I really felt cold and sick. Even if we didn't get smashed here, Maggie and I had lost the circlet—we'd never get back to where we belonged.

"Maybe you should offer them some treasures!" Igi whispered, crouched between Maggie and me. Maggie and I shrugged and poured the remaining contents of our backpacks onto the ground. There wasn't much left. A paperback horror story I'd thought I might read on the beach, a couple packs of gum, a deck of cards, and

Maggie's striped pink scarf.

"Oooo," peeped a small cluster of rocks that toddled toward us. "Soft! Soft, soft, soft."

The little thing pounced on the scarf and wrapped itself inside it. The creature bounded off, trailing rosy fluffiness behind itself.

"For shame!" growled the rocky leader. "Come back here! Rocks do not like soft. They like hard, hard, hard!"

The harsh words had no effect on the little rock, who cavorted around like a bouncing stone covered in colorful moss. But they sure set Maggie off. Hands on hips, she yelled, "What is it with you people? Where I come from, sometimes it's the youngest kid who's the smart one or the pretty one or the strong one!"

Or the brave one, I thought. But if Maggie could be brave enough to yell at the rock king, so could I. I jumped up beside her. "And sometimes it's the oldest one or the middle ones. Or maybe one is good at something and the others at something else. Why should it matter anyway where a kid is born in a family?"

"Why?" he bellowed. "Why? Because that's the way it is!"

I glanced at Maggie. She was looking at me as if she was actually proud of her big brother. I couldn't quit after that. "But it doesn't *have* to be. Things can change. I write stories. If I don't like a way a story is going, I change it. *You* can change too."

"Change is wrong! Change is evil! We will never, never change!" he roared like an avalanche. The other rock people roared the same things. I almost wished we had just shut up and let them crush us quietly.

"Change! Change! Change!" echoed around the cavern. Harsh winds began to blow, almost worse than the noise. The five of us huddled together just to keep from being knocked flat. Even the rocks seemed to be troubled by the rising wind. Most seemed to shrink into themselves, like turtles in their shells.

The echoing cries of "change" continued, high and breathy like they came from the wind itself. White sand whipped around us, stinging our skin. We all tried to bury ourselves in Doof's thick fur.

At last, the wind calmed, but the voice was still there. "Change, yesss. Change. It'sss time for change."

Slowly I raised my head, shaking off a blanket of glowing sand.

"Who said that?" I whispered. The answer blasted back.

"I did! I am Wind!"

I felt something flutter down between me and Maggie. "Zoofoo!" she cried. "Where have you been?"

The scaly little owl grinned. "When the rocks started chasing you, I flew up to get help. I found . . . *it* playing over the waves."

I must have sand in my eyes, I thought. The wind seemed to be swirling around us and taking on sort of a shape. It had arms and legs and heads, but they kept

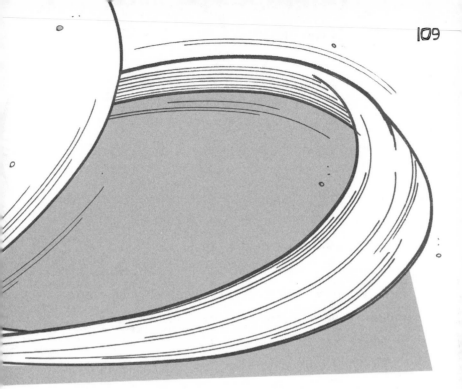

changing in number. "I *want* change. I am Wind, and winds always change. I was lonely. I wanted friends. But these creatures were s-s-soon too busy hating and fighting each other. Yes-s-s, that must change!"

The king of the rock people finally poked his head up. "But we can't change!" His roar had become more of a hoarse whisper.

Another gust of wind and we were all blown flat. Even Doof went down, setting off a great billowing of sand.

"Change! Or I will blow you all away! I am tired of s-s-seeing s-s-so much hate."

I looked around the cavern. The air filled with shifting gray sands.

"How can we change?" the rock king grumbled. "We tried before but just fought even more."

Suddenly Wind was right on top of us, like we were in the center of a hurricane. It had the loudest whisper I'd ever heard. "S-s-sometimes the oldest children are too proud. Maybe your youngest haven't learned to hate s-s-so much. Not yet. Let them try."

The Wind seemed to wrap itself around Maggie and me. "You two, an oldest and youngest—s-s-somehow you caused all this-s-s. I thank you, but you are not of our rock or sea or land or tree or sky. You should go home."

This was the scariest guy we'd met yet. I took a quavering breath and tried to answer. Maggie beat me to it: "We want to, but we can't. We've lost the things we use to travel."

She was on the verge of tears. All at once I felt more sad than scared. This was a crazier world than I had ever imagined. Sure, some of these folks, annoying as they were, had almost become our friends. But I did *not* want to be stuck away from Earth.

"Yes-s-s, those things-s-s. Lost in the s-s-sand. But s-s-sand is nothing to Wind." In a tornado of sand, Wind vanished. Almost instantly, it appeared in front of me, something silver glinting in the center of the swirling shape. With that, the creature floated away. The silver circlet and staff fell at our feet.

I sank to my knees and picked them up. "We can go home!" Maggie squealed.

I smiled broadly and looked at the others. None of them smiled back.

Igi wrapped an orange arm around my waist. "Please, don't depart our fair world! You may not be authentic tree creatures, but I will attest to your bravery. You can live with us in our splendid trees."

Nwen clutched Maggie's arm with a webbed hand. "No, with me! My folks will be nicer to you now. I may be the youngest kid, but they're going to listen to me for once!"

"No! You are land creatures," Doof grumbled. "Stay with me!"

Flapping overhead, Zoofoo squawked about her nice

mountain home. The little rock prince even mumbled something, though I couldn't quite catch it through the scarf. I could hear Wind, though, swirling more loudly around us again.

"Yeah, you all have great homes, but so do we," Maggie said. "We need to go back there."

I cleared my throat. "And anyway, your home isn't just your sea or trees or whatever. It's this whole world. Trees and ocean, sky, land, and caves. All of it. It could be a really great place if you'd stop fighting each other and just enjoy it."

As soon as I said that, I realized that our world was hardly a perfect one either. And when we had wars, we did a lot worse than throw rocks and slime at each other. But still, it was more my idea of home than this world could ever be.

Maggie took the circlet and plunked it on my head. "Lots of luck with your peace talks," Maggie called out. "And remember, power to the youngest kids!"

I thought hard about our home planet, about a world where two kids sat in a tree fort moments after having left it. The glowing sand beneath me turned into rays of light. The solid cave floor became an elevator shaft, pulling us in all directions. Then Maggie and I plopped onto a solid surface again: a flattened tree stump.

The smells and sounds of spring filled the earthly air. I took a deep breath, leaned back, and just relaxed in the warm yellow sunshine. Home. Not a perfect planet but at least one where no one was trying to eat or burn or crush us.

We laid there for minutes before Maggie finally sighed. "That was some vacation spot, big bro. But I think I know what you did wrong. Next time . . ."

"No! No *next time*. This alien gizmo is way too dangerous. From now on I'm happy to just read and write about different worlds. *Not* go visit them."

Maggie kept wheedling me, but I ignored her and crammed the circlet and the staff into my backpack. It was definitely time to be the responsible big brother.

As we walked home, sparkling white sand sifted off us like dry snow. Maggie had stopped arguing, but I could tell she was still scheming about how to try out the gizmos again. In my mind, I went over new places to hide them, places where prying little sisters would never find them.

I really should just throw them away. Sink them in the

river or toss them in a dumpster. Still, maybe I should just hide them, in case . . . No! Forget it! I can't imagine ever wanting to use these things again. But then again, imagination *is* sort of what all this is about.

And, I've got to admit, I may just have a lot of imagining left to do.

WAY-
TOO-REAL
ALIENS

#3

THE WIZARDS OF
WYRD WORLD

P. L. Cuthbertson had said he was staying at the Forest View Motel. It was almost on our way home. We made the detour. Then we headed toward the room with the parking lot's lone rental car out front.

The famous author answered the door at our second knock, wearing a rumpled blue bathrobe over his clothes. He'd probably been trying to take a nap.

"We're sorry to disturb you," Maggie said in her most polite, grown-up sounding voice. "But you said that if you could actually go to one of the worlds you write about, you'd do it."

"Sure. That's every writer's dream. But it's just that, a dream."

"It doesn't have to be," Maggie replied. "If you let us come in, we'll show you how to make it real."

P.L. shrugged. "You're writing a fantasy story? Well, come in." He ushered us in and sat on the edge of one of the twin beds. We sat on the other.

Feeling kind of stupid, I launched into an account of the blue aliens, their high-tech device, and their explanation about humans being "actualizers." Then I described what happened the last two times we'd used the gizmo.

When I'd finished, he said, "Kid, write that into a story and you're guaranteed to win the next contest."

I shook my head. "I know it sounds dumb, but it really is true. Look, here's the circlet and staff." I pulled them from my backpack. The silver circlet's three blue jewels and the short staff that plugged into them glowed in the motel lamplight.

"Cool," he commented, "but not particularly alien looking."

Then his eyes opened really wide. "That is, though." He pointed a shaking finger at the thing crawling out of my pack.

"Leggy!" I snapped. "I said you couldn't come." I glanced at P.L. He looked totally stunned and way more convinced. After all, a multi-legged, polka-dotted creature is pretty convincingly alien.

I smiled at the author. "This is a dit-dit, the little guy who came back with us from Planet Yastol. I wouldn't let him come on the last trip we made, and he's still miffed."

Maggie grabbed a cold piece of toast from a room service tray. Leggy hopped onto the table and began happily shredding it. Maggie smiled.

"Leggy's got really sharp teeth, but if he thinks you're a friend of Josh's, he won't do that to you."

P.L. gulped. "Right. Josh, you're my new best friend." Then he laughed. "You had me fooled for a moment, but I guess that's some sort of remote-controlled thing."

I shook my head. "Nobody controls Leggy."

Maggie grabbed the circlet out of my hand and smiled at the author. "Let's make a deal. You put this on and let us stick in the staff. If nothing happens, fine. We'll take Leggy and head back home. But if it works, you hold our hands so we can come along to Wyrd World with you."

He laughed. "Deal. On the condition that you let me use this idea in one of my next books. It's got potential."

"Deal," Maggie and I both said, smiling.

That was the last time any of us smiled for quite a while.

ABOUT THE AUTHOR

Pamela F. Service has written more than thirty books in the science fiction, fantasy, and nonfiction genres. After working as a history museum curator for many years in Indiana, she became the director of a museum in Eureka, California, where she lives with her husband and cats. She is also active in community theater, politics, and beachcombing.

ABOUT THE ILLUSTRATOR

Mike Gorman is a seasoned editorial illustrator whose work has been seen in the *New York Times*, the *New Yorker*, *Entertainment Weekly*, and other publications. He is also the illustrator of the Alien Agent series. He lives in Westbrook, Maine, with his wife, three children, a dog, a cat, two toads, and a gecko.